Lewy Kablooey
& Sneezy
Cheezy

by CINDY STEWART

◆ FriesenPress

Suite 300 - 990 Fort St
Victoria, BC, V8V 3K2
Canada

www.friesenpress.com

Copyright © 2017 by Cindy Stewart
First Edition — 2017

Ilustrator: Natalia Starikova

ISBN
978-1-5255-0069-5 (Paperback)
978-1-5255-0070-1 (eBook)

1. JUVENILE FICTION, FANTASY & MAGIC

Distributed to the trade by The Ingram Book Company

Dedicated, in loving memory, to my husband, Lewis Stewart and my mother, Dorothy Penny.

Thank you for all your love and encouragement to follow my dreams!

LEWY KABLOOEY & SNEEZY CHEEZY

Lewy's mom cautiously poked her head into the garage. She was a short woman with light coloured hair, and she was very motherly, quiet, and kind.

"Lewy, would you please go to the store for a loaf of bread?"

Lewy was also short, wore glasses, and was a bit plump. His fondness toward animals added to his sweet disposition.

"Look out Mom!" Lewy hollered.

His robot Rodney came to an abrupt stop at his mother's feet. As its bottle cap eyes stared up at Lewy's mom its arms suddenly fell off onto the floor.

"Sure, I can go to the store," Lewy said. "I'll ride my Star Traveller."

"Remember it really doesn't fly," said his mom.

Lewy built the Star Traveller sort of like a go-cart. The frame was made from a plank of wood with four bicycle wheels attached. He used a wooden crate for the front, and fastened an old lawnmower engine and a fan blade to the back. He made the wings by gluing some canvas to old window frames, and spray-painted *Star Traveller* on the front with a few stars for good luck.

Lewy took a deep breath then pulled the lawnmower cord. When the engine started, it turned the belt that made the rear wheels spin. The wings started flapping as he pulled the broom handle lever attached to a clothesline and pulley. For a split second the wheels left the ground!

Shocked, he caught a glimpse of Johnny and Herbie watching from across the street.

But as fast as he had lifted off, his invention came crashing to the ground.

"Lewy just give up!" shouted Johnny.

"Yeah, all of your inventions go kablooey!" laughed Herbie.

Johnny was tall and stocky with dark coloured hair. Herbie was slender and known for his red hair and freckles.

Embarrassed, Lewy scooted off the Star Traveller and ran to the store. When he got back a crowd of kids had gathered.

"Lewy Kablooey! Lewy Kablooey!" they all chanted.

Bread in hand, Lewy pushed the Star Traveller through the crowd and back into the garage and quickly shut the door.

"Ah-choo!"

"Who's there?" Lewy said.

"AH-CHOOOOOOO!"

Lewy nervously switched on the lights. His eyes were drawn to a rather large, calico cat perched on his workbench and staring out with stunning, green, saucer-shaped eyes.

Astonished, he rushed the loaf of bread to his mom and promptly returned to the garage.

"Who are you?" Lewy stared at the cat. "Where did you come from?"

The enormous cat sneezed again, spraying Rodney from head to toe.

Lewy cringed as he wiped off his robot.

"That's it! I'll call you Sneezy and I definitely need to teach you how to use a tissue.

Wait, what's this around your neck?"

The cat had a collar with a tag that looked like a cube of cheese.

"Are you sure you don't think you're a mouse?" Lewy chuckled. "Even better, your name will be Sneezy Cheezy!"

Lewy's dad approached the garage. "Time for bed, Lewy!"

"Good night, Sneezy Cheezy. I'll fetch you some food and water before I go to sleep."

* * *

In the morning, Lewy found Sneezy Cheezy strangely intrigued with his blueprints for a futuristic ice cream parlour in outer space.

"I need to go to school, Sneezy. I'll see you when I get back."

On the way to class Lewy noticed a sign-up sheet hanging outside the science classroom. It was for the Science Fair on Saturday.

Johnny and Herbie were lingering nearby, waiting to tease him, but Lewy ignored them as he wrote,

"Lewy Brown, Invention: The Star Traveller."

Later that day, Lewy passed by the sign-up sheet. He noticed that *Brown* had been scratched out and *Kablooey* was written in its place. He walked by not giving Johnny and Herbie the flustered reaction they wanted.

After school, Lewy ran home to feed Sneezy Cheezy. He grabbed some food from the

fridge and raced back to his workshop.

"Don't spoil your dinner, Lewy," said his mom.

Lewy started on the repairs to his Star Traveller.

"You can do it!"

Astonished, Lewy gazed at Sneezy. "You talk?"

Sneezy grinned. "All the cats from Planet Cheese talk!"

"What are you doing on Earth?" asked Lewy.

Sneezy whimpered. "My Cheddar Ship crashed and it's beyond repair. I saw your Star Traveller and thought you could help me get back to my planet."

Lewy reached out and hugged Sneezy. "I can try."

Saturday arrived and Sneezy went with Lewy to the Science Fair. The judge asked Lewy to demonstrate the Star Traveller. He climbed aboard with Sneezy in tow.

He started the engine. Sweat formed on his brow as he started the wings in motion.

Sneezy whispered, "Believe in yourself!"

The Star Traveller lifted off the ground. The crowd cheered as Lewy and Sneezy buzzed overhead.

Sneezy smiled. "Congratulations Lewy!"

Just then, Sneezy started sneezing endlessly into the fuel tank.

Lewy looked at Sneezy with disbelief. "You could have made my invention fly for me?"

"That's something you had to do for yourself, Lewy Kablooey!" said Sneezy.

Before Sneezy soared away in the Star Traveller, he brought Lewy down to receive his first-place trophy.

That night the stars in the sky spelled out

Friends Forever!

Born in Hamilton, Ontario, **Cindy** has always had a passion for writing. In 2002, she and her husband, Lewis Stewart, moved to a farm in Dunnville. They have three sons, Ryan, Shawn, and Kevin; two granddaughters, Madison and Alexis; and many animal friends.

Lew was a genius at creating and repairing things, and the family cat, Cheezy, always nearby, had a cold and was often sneezing when Cindy was writing this story. She also remembers her husband telling her about how he was bullied as a child, and now that Lew and Cheezy have both passed away, this book is even closer to her heart.

Children and animals have always held a special place in Cindy's life. She has volunteered at the Doors of Friendship Community School, coached East End T-Ball, and worked with the Friends of the Aviary, all located in Hamilton. She shared much of her volunteer work with her husband, and together they also visited children with their farm animals.

Cindy enjoyed a thirty-year career with the Hamilton Wentworth District School Board, twenty of which were at Parkdale Elementary School. There she found a second home, working with students, and relaying the message that they should always believe in themselves.

She also directed the Parkdale School choir, empowering her students every step of the way.

Now retired, Cindy hopes to continue the inspiring messages that run through **Lewy Kablooey & Sneezy Cheezy**, as well as creating more inspiring books in the future.

CPSIA information can be obtained
at www.ICGtesting.com
Printed in the USA
BVHW091215040321
601645BV00002B/5